Picture Book of Classic

中国传统故事美绘本（中英文双语版）

花木兰

Hua Mulan

在中国南北朝时期，有一位巾帼英雄，她的名字叫花木兰。

木兰出生在北方的一个小乡村，父亲是退役军人，母亲勤劳善良。木兰还有一个年纪相仿的姐姐和一个年幼的弟弟。一家人辛勤劳作，虽不富裕，但生活幸福。

In the Northern and Southern Dynasties of China (420-589) lived a heroine, named Hua Mulan.

Born in a small village in northern China, Mulan lived with her veteran father, her hard-working and kind-hearted mother, her elder sister and a younger brother. The whole family managed to lead a happy, if not wealthy, life through their hard work.

木兰从小喜欢使刀弄枪,父亲一有空就带她到村外的小河边,教她练武,骑马、射箭、舞刀、使棒,样样都练。别看她是个女孩子,一点儿也不比男孩子差。而且,经过父亲的指导,木兰到十五岁时,十八般武艺样样精通,方圆百里没人是她的对手。木兰还喜欢没事就翻看父亲的旧兵书,从中学到很多兵法兵略。木兰聪明伶俐,又勤劳善良,邻里都很喜欢她。

From childhood Mulan had taken great interest in the life of a warrior. During their spare time, her father trained her in fighting skills at the riverside nearby, everything from riding horses to shooting arrows, from swinging a broadsword to wielding a staff. Though she was a girl, she was the equal of a man in the skills she developed. Thanks to her father's training, Mulan had mastered the various combat skills by the age of fifteen, and no one who lived nearby was her match. Also, Mulan liked to read her father's old books about the art of war, from which she acquired much knowledge about military skills and strategies.

As Mulan was a smart, lively, diligent and nice girl, all her neighbors adored.

这天，木兰练剑回到家，见父亲紧锁愁眉，母亲也唉声叹气。木兰担心起来，这段时间北方番兵南下，侵略国境，边境形势紧张，人心惶惶。她赶紧问："爹，出什么事了？"父亲见了木兰，只是叹气不语。母亲说："朝廷要征兵打仗了，十二卷军书，每卷都有你爹的名字，可你爹现在体弱多病，咱家又无适龄男丁，这可如何是好？"是啊，父亲日渐衰老，弟弟太年幼，才八岁，木兰和姐姐又是女孩，怎么办呢？

One day, after Mulan had finished her swordsmanship practice, she went back home only to find something unusual. Her father seemed anxious, with furrowed brows, and her mother was moaning and groaning. Mulan was immediately worried, thinking of the recent border skirmishes. Recently the Huns had begun to invade the border, and the northern boundary was at risk. People lived in panic. Then Mulan asked, "Dad, what happened?"

Without answering, Mulan's father only heaved a great sigh. Her mother said, "The Emperor is calling up soldiers. Twelve conscription notices have been delivered, each one with your Dad's name on it. But your father is ailing and no one else is available; what should we do?" Yes, it was tough. Father was aging. Brother was only an eight-year old child. Mulan and her sister could not be chosen. What could they do?

木兰坐在织布机前，心不在焉地摆弄着织布机，半天也没织出一块布。姐姐见木兰愁眉苦脸直叹气，就拉上她到屋外给两只兔子喂食。木兰见姐姐边喂边指着其中一只兔子说："估计明年就能生下几个兔宝宝了吧？"木兰很奇怪，问姐姐："你怎么知道这只是母兔呢？没准儿两只都是公兔呢？"姐姐说："当然啊，我天天喂养它们，自然分得清楚。不过，从外观看起来，这两只兔子没什么差别，别人可分不清！"听了姐姐的话，木兰眼睛一亮，一个大胆想法突然在她脑中闪现，她拉着姐姐就朝屋里跑去。

Sitting in front of the loom, Mulan meant to weave, but her mind kept wandering and no weaving got done for a long time. Seeing Mulan's worried look, her sister took her out of the room to feed their animals. "She may have babies next year," her sister said, pointing to one of their two rabbits.

"How do you know this is a female rabbit? Perhaps both of them are males," said Mulan.

"Of course I know. I have fed them for a long time, so I can separate the female from the male easily. But judging by their looks alone, others can't tell which is which." Her sister's words lit up Mulan's mind like a flash, and she rushed back to the house, dragging her sister along.

木兰问父亲:"爹,女儿的武艺怎么样?""我女儿的武艺超群,即使男子也不是我女儿的对手呢!"父亲自豪地说道。"嗯,嗯。"母亲、姐姐和弟弟也点头同意。"所以,我要代父从军。"木兰一脸严肃地说道。母亲首先吓了一跳,姐姐也觉得不可思议,弟弟更是对木兰说道:"阿姐,你没开玩笑吧! 你是一个女子,朝廷征兵要求是男子!"木兰斩钉截铁地说:"如果我女扮男装,有谁知道我是一个女子呢?"

　　"不行,"父亲严肃地说道,"战场凶险难测,非同儿戏啊!"

　　"爹,娘,木兰心意已决,望你们成全。爹爹年老体弱,怎经得起战场的艰辛。我虽为女儿身,但一直羡慕男儿豪气干云,且我常有报国之志,此次若能奔赴边疆报效国家,也不辜负了我的一身好武艺。"

"How are my combat skills, Dad?" Mulan asked her father in the house.

　　"My daughter's combat skills are outstanding. She even outperforms men!" her father said proudly. And her mother, sister and brother also nodded yes.

　　"So, then, I plan to take Dad's place in the army," Mulan announced in a grave voice.

　　Her mother was taken aback; her sister felt it unimaginable and her brother said to her, "Sister, are you kidding? You are a girl. Soldiers are men!"

　　"If I disguise myself as a man, who will know?" Mulan asserted.

　　"No way," her father said seriously. "The battlefield is full of unexpected dangers, not a place for fun!"

　　"Dad, Mom, I have made up my mind on the plan. Please let it be. Dad's health is failing; how can he manage the rigors of battle. I'm a girl, but I have always admired men's strength and heroism. I wish to serve my country. If I can join the army, all my efforts in skills training will be worthwhile, " Mulan said.

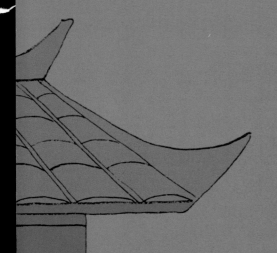

父亲见女儿这般坚决，也只好同意。第二天，木兰即到集市，买了马匹、盔甲和武器等装备。木兰束上头发，穿上战袍，披上盔甲，骑上战马，英姿飒爽——好一个英俊的男子！父亲告诫木兰："你要记住，走路时，步伐要大；说话时，声音要粗；在人前，要昂首挺胸，显出一副男子气概。"木兰将父亲的话谨记在心。

Mulan was so resolute that her father had to agree. The next day, she went to the market to buy herself a horse and some gear. Binding up her long hair, putting on the armor, mounting the steed—Mulan transformed herself into a handsome young man!

"Mulan, remember, it is time to show your manliness: steps big; voice rough; shoulders back and chest high," her father told her. Mulan kept all of it in mind.

这天早上天刚露微白,木兰便辞别父母姐弟,骑上骏马,奔赴战场。马蹄声急,重山如飞。夜宿黄河边,晚风清冷,只听黄河流水哗哗。第二天离开黄河,继续前行,暮至黑山头,天黑山高,森然可怖,偶尔传来燕山胡兵的战马嘶鸣——离战场不远了。木兰毫无畏惧,加快速度直奔军营。

One morning at daybreak, Mulan bid farewell to her family and headed for the battlefield, riding on her warhorse. The steed's hoof beats echoed off the surrounding hills and soon the mountains had fallen behind them. That evening Mulan rested next to the Yellow River where

e night breeze felt cold and the running water was gurgling.
he next day Mulan left the Yellow River and moved on. At
sk she arrived at Heishan Mountain where the overwhelm-
g darkness was filled with unseen terrors, and the occasion-
neighing of horses could be heard from afar. It was obvi-
s to Mulan that she was approaching the battlefield.
t in the least afraid, Mulan increased
r pace, heading for the army's camp.

作战训练，木兰不怕艰苦，意志坚强；对敌阵前，木兰英勇奋战，毫不畏惧；行军打仗，木兰足智多谋，屡立战功。士兵们佩服木兰武艺高强，将军欣赏木兰有勇有谋，木兰从一名普通士兵很快成长为一名将领，和战士们同甘共苦，同仇敌忾。多年来，将士们驰骋疆场，历经百战，死伤无数，终于彻底败退敌人，得以胜利归来。

　　Joining the military training, Mulan went through various hardships, fortified by her strong willpower. Fighting against the Hun soldiers, she distinguished herself. Being clever, Mulan contributed a lot to the defeats over the enemy. Other soldiers admired Mulan for her skill in battle, and the general appreciated her for her courage and intelligence. As a result, Mulan was soon appointed a high-ranking officer and spent the remainder of the bitter war leading soldiers in battle. The war lasted for many years and claimed many lives, but finally the Huns were totally defeated and the army returned home in triumph.

木兰回朝拜见天子，天子论功行赏，见木兰军功煊赫，便赐木兰高官厚爵，但木兰婉言谢绝，她不爱高官，也不爱厚爵，她禀告天子：征战边疆垂，十年使得归；家人音书断，思亲想断肠；名禄转眼逝，唯情长久远；愿骑千里马，送我回故乡。天子被这个不重名利的军人所感动，赐予千金，恩准木兰回乡与家人团聚。

　　The Emperor met the triumphantly returning army and rewarded them according to their deeds. As Mulan had made great contributions to the victory, the Emperor awarded her a high position and a handsome sum of money. Interested in neither power nor wealth, however, Mulan turned it down. Instead, she said to the Emperor, "Your Majesty, after fighting in the remote regions for over ten years, I have finally returned. But having lost contact with my family for so long, I have missed them sorely. Power and wealth only last for a while, but my love for my family is forever. What I want is simple, a swift horse to carry me home as quickly as possible." The Emperor was moved by Mulan's words and actions and, after presenting her with a rich reward of money, agreed to her request to return immediately to her hometown.

　　木兰衣锦还乡的消息传遍了家乡的每个角落。父母年纪大了,腿脚不好,但听说女儿要回来了,不禁感激涕零,互相搀扶着到城外迎接她;阿姐听说阿妹回来了,赶紧整理衣装,在门口翘首盼望;阿弟听说阿姐要回来,赶紧忙着磨刀霍霍,杀猪宰羊,为阿姐接风。

The news of Mulan's return soon spread all over her hometown. Her aged parents could not withhold their heartfelt tears any more when they heard the news. Eager to see Mulan as soon as possible, they supported one another as they hurried out into the countryside to meet her, buoyed by their joy though they were, in fact, much too old to manage such a long walk. Mulan's sister dressed herself up to greet Mulan at the door. As for the little brother, knowing that Mulan was coming back, he hurried to sharpen the knife to slaughter the cattle in order to prepare a feast for his sister.

木兰回到家,家里一切如昨,只是爹娘苍老了,弟弟长大了。木兰入屋脱下战袍,换上一袭长裙,又面对铜镜,梳理长发,插上玉簪,薄施粉黛,一身女儿装束,方才盈盈而出。同行打仗的伙伴们目瞪口呆——与木兰一同征战十数年,竟然不知木兰是个女孩!

千百年来,人们对木兰代父从军、忠孝两全、舍身报国的精神敬佩不已。

Mulan returned home to find that everyone had changed a great deal. Her parents were getting older. Her brother had grown up. Back in her own room, Mulan took off her armor and put on a dress. Sitting in front of the bronze mirror, she tidied her hair and pinned it up with her old hairpin. Then she used a bit of makeup. She carefully adorned herself for a long time before she emerged in full elegance. All her fellow soldiers were stunned by her presence—fighting with Mulan for more than ten years, no one had expected that "he" would turn out to be a beauty!

The story of Mulan's replacing her father in the army is passed on from generation to generation. People of different times all deeply admire Mulan for her self-giving love for her family and her nation.

完

End